JEASY

Weiss, Ellen, 1949-

My first day at camp /
1999.